The Itch in a Hitch

The Itch in a Hitch

AND OTHER HUMOROUS STORIES
Compiled by the Editors
of
Highlights for Children

Compilation copyright © 1994 by Highlights for Children, Inc.
Contents copyright by Highlights for Children, Inc.
Published by Highlights for Children, Inc.
P.O. Box 18201
Columbus, Ohio 43218-0201
Printed in the United States of America

ISBN: 0-87534-626-X

Highlights˚ is a registered trademark of Highlights for Children, Inc.

CONTENTS

The Itch in a Hitch

By Marilyn Bissell

"Are you sure you'll be all right if we leave you alone?" asked Mrs. Ames.

"I'm positive, Mom," said Nancy. She was used to the cast on her leg and got around quite well with her crutches. Besides, it would be no fun to sit and watch everyone else skate at the roller rink. Dad had promised Nancy's sister, Kathy, a skating party on her birthday. At the time, no one had expected Nancy to have a broken leg.

"You can borrow my Mexican jumping beans while I'm gone," said Kathy, handing Nancy the tiny grayish beans.

"Thanks," said Nancy.

"And here's some bubble gum," said Nancy's brother, Tom. They were trying to comfort her, she knew, but she wouldn't really feel better until the doctor removed the cast the following day. The weeks had dragged by since she had skateboarded off a ramp and broken her leg. Never again! No more stunts like that!

After the family left, Nancy looked down at the beans in her hand. Kathy claimed there were little worms inside that moved when they were warm, causing the beans to jump. They were motionless now. She closed her hand to warm them. Nothing.

Suddenly, her healing leg began to itch. She reached to scratch it and—oops! The beans dropped inside the heavy cast. In moments, they began to jump. And jump. And jump.

Nancy's mom had given her a long knitting needle to use for scratching her leg. She carefully slid the slender tip of the needle inside the cast and poked at the beans. They jumped even more.

"I have to get those beans out, or I'll go bonkers," Nancy said to herself. The beans were doing a Mexican hat dance now.

Nancy looked around her room for something that might retrieve the annoying beans from the depths of her cast. As she blew a bubble that stuck to her face, an idea came to her. The gum!

She stuck the gooey wad of gum to the tip of the needle. Carefully, she slid the needle inside the cast, aiming at the dancing beans. It had almost reached its target when the beans gave a jump and Nancy flinched. The gum dropped off the needle and sank to the bottom of the cast. Now Nancy not only had the beans doing a flamenco dance in there but she also had a sticky mess clinging to her leg.

She had to do something! The itching was becoming unbearable. Tucking her crutches under her arms, Nancy hobbled to the kitchen. In the cupboard she found a jar of molasses. Nothing could be stickier. She dipped the tip of the needle in the molasses and poked it into the cast. The molasses dripped from the needle and coated her leg, but the beans danced on. They were doing the hustle now.

Nancy hobbled into the backyard and sank onto the chaise lounge under the apple tree. "Now what am I going to do?" she wondered. "I wish I could stand on my head and make those beans fall out!"

Nancy realized that standing on her head was out of the question. But wouldn't it be possible, just maybe, to tip up her leg with the cast on it until the beans fell out?

As the beans began to disco, Nancy noticed Kathy's jump rope lying on the ground beside her chair. That was it! She'd make a pulley. She tied one end of the rope to her ankle and tried to toss the other end over the tree branch above her head. The rope finally wound itself over the branch. Nancy grasped the dangling end and, leaning back in the chair, began to pull.

With each tug on the rope, Nancy's ankle rose higher into the air, lifting the heavy cast. Harder and harder she pulled until she was lying flat with her foot aimed toward the sky. The beans danced. The gum stuck stubbornly in place. And the molasses began to run slowly toward her knee.

"One more tug should do it," thought Nancy. She held the rope tightly and gave a mighty pull. Apples fell like rain, pelting her face, as the branch snapped and crashed from the tree. Her leg dropped with a thud. The lawn chair tipped and she fell facedown on the grass. The beans shifted inside the cast and began to rhumba. Nancy was ready to scream.

She lay on the grass for a few minutes, exhausted. When she finally rolled over, she noticed that a colony of tiny black ants had discovered the stream of molasses and was following it into the cast. The beans were dancing *La Cucaracha*.

Just then the family returned from the skating expedition. Nancy's mother gasped when she saw her. Kathy wanted her jumping beans, and Tom asked if there was any gum left. Nancy's father was the only one who noticed the ants, the broken branch, and the rope attached to Nancy's ankle. He listened carefully as Nancy explained what had happened.

The doctor, wearing tennis clothes, was not pleased with the emergency call to his office. But he agreed to remove the cast a day early. Soon Nancy's itching leg was freed. There was the hardened gum. There was the swarm of ants feasting on molasses. And there were the Mexican jumping beans performing a cha-cha.

Nancy scooped up the beans and put them in her pocket before she slid down from the examining table. She would return them to Kathy as soon as she got home. She never wanted to see them again as long as she lived.

Mr. McMuddle's Troubles

By Juanita Barrett Friedrichs

One morning when Mr. McMuddle climbed out of bed, he found he was out of clean socks.

"I'll just have to wear a dirty pair," he said. He pulled the pile of dirty socks from under his bed.

"Uh-oh!"

Mr. McMuddle let go of the socks in a hurry and jumped on his bed. There was an ugly something-or-other sitting in the pile of socks, blinking at him.

"You woke me up," it growled.

"Wh-what *are* you?" stuttered Mr. McMuddle.

"I'm an Ickirag, of course."

"Icky is right," gasped Mr. McMuddle. He ran out of the room in his bare feet and snuck into the quiet kitchen.

"I need a cup of hot cocoa," he said, "to calm my nerves."

But there were no more clean cups in his cupboard. They were all piled in the sink.

"Oh, fiddle fuddle," sighed Mr. McMuddle. "I will have to wash a cup." He sprinkled soap powder on the dirty dishes.

Someone gave a loud sneeze.

"Quit sprinkling me with that disgusting stuff!"

Mr. McMuddle almost fell over. A horrible something-or-other was sitting in his cocoa cup.

"Wh-what *are* you?" stammered Mr. McMuddle.

"I'm a Jugalump, of course. I was soaking my feet—KERCHOO!—in the cocoa you left in this cup. Last week's cocoa is very good for sore feet."

Mr. McMuddle decided he didn't need cocoa. He tiptoed into the living room and squeezed himself onto the sofa between piles of old junk he had been saving. To calm his nerves, he wrote his name backward on the coffee table. The dust was so thick that his finger made a good pencil.

Then he heard a creaking noise over his head. He looked up. Near the ceiling in one of the corners was an old ragged cobweb. The cobweb was swinging back and forth. Someone was using it as a hammock.

"Who invited *you?*" yelled Mr. McMuddle.

"*You* invited me," said a mean-sounding voice. Two mean-looking eyes peered over the edge of the cobweb. "With all of these empty hammocks in your house, I thought you wanted guests."

"I do not," said Mr. McMuddle. "And who *are* you, anyway?"

"I'm an Ughabug, of course. I've tried every hammock on this ceiling, and they're all terrible. They all creak or squeak. Now leave me alone so I can sleep."

Mr. McMuddle was glad to get out of the living room. "But where shall I go?" he wondered. "Every room in my house has some horrible creature in it."

Mr. McMuddle went out and sat on his porch. It was raining. The roof leaked right over his chair.

"I want my house back," sobbed Mr. McMuddle. Then he thought for a while. "I'll *get* it back, too!"

Mr. McMuddle stomped into his house and headed for the broom closet. He began to swing his broom and swish his dustcloth everywhere.

When the Ickirag, the Jugalump, and the Ughabug saw Mr. McMuddle cleaning house, they all screamed and ran out the back door.

Mr. McMuddle washed and folded his dirty clothes and put them away. He scrubbed his dirty dishes and stacked them in the kitchen cupboard.

Then he threw out the junk he had been saving—
the used-up ketchup bottles and broken chairs
and shoes with holes in them.

The house was almost empty!

Mr. McMuddle felt very proud of himself. And
very tired. "I think I will take a nap," he said. He
climbed into his clean bed.

But soon Mr. McMuddle heard scraping noises.
He opened his eyes. "Oh, no!" he groaned.

A whole army of ugly-looking something-or-
others was moving into his bedroom. What was
worse, they were dragging suitcases and boxes
behind them.

"Who invited *you?*" yelled Mr. McMuddle.

"Ickirag, Jugalump, and Ughabug told us about
your place," the something-or-others yelled back.
"When we hear of an empty house, we move in.
We bring our own stuff."

Mr. McMuddle jumped out of bed. "Hold it,
you—you—"

"Jamablanks, if you please. Now don't disturb
us while we unpack. We will be ready for supper
in a little while."

"THIS IS NOT A HOTEL!" roared Mr. McMuddle.

He went into his clean living room to think
things over. "When my house was full of junk and
dirt, the Ickirag, the Jugalump, and the Ughabug
moved in. Now that my house is clean and empty,
I'm stuck with Jamablanks."

16

Suddenly Mr. McMuddle knew what was wrong. His house was *too* empty. He went out to his yard and looked at all of the junk he had left outside for the garbage man.

"No," he said to himself. "I don't want that old junk back. I need something different."

Mr. McMuddle made a list of things he needed. Then he went shopping.

By the time he got home, Mr. McMuddle could hardly squeeze through his front door. His house was jammed with Jamablanks.

"Where is our dinner?" yelled the Jamablanks.

"Out of my way!" roared Mr. McMuddle. He pulled up the shades. He opened the windows. "We're going to have plenty of sunshine and fresh air in this house!"

"Yuck!" muttered the Jamablanks.

Then Mr. McMuddle carried in everything he had bought on his shopping trip.

"We're going to have bright colors on the walls," he said firmly. "And fresh flowers on the table. And curtains with yellow polka dots. And towels with red stripes. And blue dishes. And . . ."

"Stop, stop!" groaned the Jamablanks.

"And a canary that sings all day long."

"That does it!" screeched the Jamablanks. "Sunshine and fresh air are bad enough. Colors and flowers are worse. But a canary that sings is JUST TOO MUCH!"

There was a terrible scurrying and scampering. There was a horrible scraping and scratching. All the Jamablanks rushed out the back door. They dragged their belongings behind them.

Mr. McMuddle hung the canary cage near a sunny window. Then he went right to work, while the canary sang.

Soon Mr. McMuddle's house was the prettiest, most cheerful house in town. It was far too clean for Ickirags, Jugalumps, and Ughabugs. It was much too nice for Jamablanks. And it has been that way ever since.

THREE-ALARM
IN THE
FIREHOUSE

By Joan Knaub

Sam Soupe was the new firehouse cook. He came to work one morning with shiny pans, big black skillets, long ladles, and a white chef's hat with a fireman's brim.

"Hi, Sam! What's for dinner?" called Tiny Tom Tuttle, who stood six feet and seven inches in his black boots.

"Stew," said Sam briefly. He didn't like to be bothered when he was working.

"Something smells good!" exclaimed Big Billy Baines a few minutes later. "What is it?"

"Stew," snapped Sam, clattering his pans.

"Mmm," sniffed Jolly Joe Johnson when he ambled through the kitchen. "What's cooking?"

"Stew!" shouted Sam, tired of all the interruptions.

Tiny Tom, Big Billy, and Jolly Joe sat outside the dining room, rubbing their stomachs. It was still an hour before dinner.

"Hope Sam's a good cook," said Tiny Tom.

"Me, too," sighed Big Billy.

"Remember the last cook?" moaned Jolly Joe. "Everything tasted as flat as desert sand."

"Let's cross our fingers and hope that Sam can season things," said Tom.

"Guess I'll go polish the brass on number 6 engine," said Big Billy, "and wait to see what kind of meal Sam puts on."

"I'll grease the fire pole until the dinner bell sounds," said Jolly Joe.

"And I'll check the hoses for leaks," said Tom.

All was quiet in the firehouse. Sam was in his quarters clipping recipes, and in the kitchen the stew simmered merrily on the stove. The equipment that Sam had brought with him sat silent and shiny—spoons and spatulas, pans and pots, racks of spices, and a set of salt-and-pepper shakers.

Tiny Tom tiptoed into the quiet kitchen. "I do hanker after a lively stew," he thought as he shook the pepper shaker hard over the bubbling kettle. Silently he glided out.

Stretching his arms, Big Billy came into the kitchen for a drink of water. "Wonder if the stew is seasoned properly?" Billy twitched his nose and decided it wasn't. Vigorously he spattered pepper. And whistling, he sauntered out.

Jolly Joe came into the kitchen to see if Sam had left any snacks. There was nothing on the counter, but Joe sniffed hungrily at the good smell of stew. "It just might need pepping up. Guess it won't hurt if I add a pinch of pepper." Joe shook the shaker so hard that he sneezed. "That ought to do it," he said in a satisfied way.

Sam came down a few minutes before dinner. He checked the table, crisp and clean with a white cloth, and set with bowls, silverware, napkins, and milk. Sam nodded. Fine! He added a big plate of crackers and went to get the stew.

"And for the final touch—" Sam delicately grasped the pepper shaker and gave seven mighty shakes. Then he sounded the dinner bell, and the men filed in. Stew was ladled into deep bowls, and the men took up their spoons.

"Ahghhh!"

"Help!"

"Yuck!"

"Ulp!"

Everyone, including Sam, was jumping around holding his throat.

"Water, water!" croaked Big Billy.

"The little hose on engine 4!" gasped Tom.

"Hurry, hurry!" urged Joe in a hoarse whisper.

The men got to the engine, but in their haste to pull out the hose, they hit the alarm and the bell began to clang. They were too busy cooling their tongues to stop it. But finally Big Billy reached up and turned it off.

In the silence that followed, Tiny Tom said, "Guess I added a shade too much pepper."

"'Spect I did, too," admitted Jolly Joe.

Big Billy grinned sheepishly. "I added my shake or two."

"Well!" Sam Soupe was furious. "So you don't think I'm a good enough cook, is that it? I know enough not to stay where I'm not wanted. My bags are as good as packed."

"Sam, Sam," pleaded Tom and Billy and Joe together. "Stay, please stay. We promise that never, never will we interfere with your cooking. Give us one more chance."

Sam thought for a minute. "All right," he decided, "one more chance. But I hope you remember that too many cooks—"

"Can start a three-alarm fire!" shouted the men.

And Sam Soupe smiled the only smile that the firehouse gang would ever get to see on his thin, narrow lips.

Dilly and the Dream Scheme

By Kathleen Stevens

The creak of the bedroom door woke me. A beam of light hit my face. My sister whispered, "Nate, tell me what you were dreaming."

"Dilly! What's going on?"

"Sh-h-h. You'll wake up J.P." Dilly sat on my bed, balancing a notepad on her knees. "Hold the flashlight while I write."

"Write what?"

"Your dream. I am doing an experiment for my science class to show that outside stimuli get included in our dreams."

"Outside what?"

"Lights. Noises. Stuff like that. Now, tell me about your dream. Did you see a bright light in it?"

"I wasn't even dreaming."

Dilly was disgusted. "How can I write up my experiment if you weren't dreaming?"

"Sorry, Dilly," I said sarcastically. "Next time I'll do better."

"OK, Nate. I'll try again." Dilly took the flashlight and walked out of the room.

"Hey!" I yelped. "I was just kidding. Don't you dare wake me up again—ever—for any of your foolish experiments."

But Dilly was gone. Groaning, I closed my eyes. Another of Dilly's projects was launched.

Dilly's inventive ideas have bothered our family for years. It started when she was four and was still called Dolores. While Mom and a neighbor were having coffee, the neighbor's little girl played with Dilly and me. A clown on TV demonstrated how he put on his makeup. Impressed, my sister pulled out her markers and went to work on the three of us.

The neighbor wasn't pleased with her child's decorated face. "That girl of yours is a dilly," she said. We've called Dolores "Dilly" ever since.

After Dilly started school, things got worse. Other kids go to the library and write reports. Dilly always adds a creative touch of her own.

My dad remembers Dilly's Viking report. Dilly insisted on visiting the Viking exhibit at the art museum, and Dad had to drive her. "I'll look real fast," Dilly assured him, so Dad parked at a thirty-minute meter. An hour later, he had to drag Dilly away from the museum—and found a parking ticket under the windshield wiper.

Mom remembers the time Dilly cut up three of our best sheets to make Roman togas. To build a Cape Cod house for social studies, Dilly used J.P.'s collection of Popsicle sticks. And she ruined my baseball glove by covering it with papier-mâché. "I'm sorry, Nate," she apologized. "I wanted a model for my art project. I thought this stuff would peel off."

"Dilly," I told her, "leave me and my belongings out of your projects."

Did she listen? Not Dilly. Now we had to live with her wild dream scheme.

The following night I woke to see Dilly next to J.P.'s bed—the flashlight beamed on his face. J.P. blinked sleepily.

"What were you dreaming?" Dilly demanded.

"Nothing," J.P. mumbled. He flopped over on his stomach and went right back to sleep.

Dilly gave an exasperated sigh, then looked at my bed.

"Oh, no you don't—I'm already awake, Dilly!" I whispered angrily.

"Nate," she said, "what am I going to do? I haven't found any examples of outside stimuli in people's dreams."

"I don't care what you do," I told her. "Just don't shine lights in my face."

Dilly was silent for a moment. "OK, Nate. No more lights."

It wasn't a light that woke me the next night. It was cold water.

"A-a-arg!" I lurched upright in bed. Dilly stood beside me, a glass in her hand.

Mom burst into the bedroom, Dad behind her. "What happened? Nate, are you OK?"

Dilly realized she'd gone too far. "I didn't mean to disturb everybody. I was just trickling water on Nate's face."

"Trickling?" I retorted. "You threw a whole glassful at me."

"I wanted to make sure you'd feel it," Dilly explained. "My experiments haven't been working well." Dilly began to tell them, in great detail, about her dream project.

"I'm going back to bed," Dad groaned.

"We all are. You had better get moving, Dilly," Mom ordered.

Dilly leaned closer to my bed. "Nate, did you dream it was raining?"

"No," I growled. "I dreamed it was hailing pillows!" I heaved mine at Dilly.

"We've got to do something about her," J.P. muttered as Dilly left.

He was right. We had to teach Dilly a lesson. Mom and Dad agreed.

The next night Mom woke us. We gathered in the dark, J.P. toting his drum, Dad carrying a horn from New Year's Eve, and Mom holding a whistle. I had two big pot lids.

"Ready?" Dad whispered as we reached Dilly's door. "Go!"

We burst into Dilly's room, and Mom flipped the light switch. J.P. thumped, Mom blew, Dad tooted, and I clanged. We sounded terrific—like a dump truck unloading scrap iron.

Dilly lurched up in bed, staring at us.

"A taste of your own torture!" I announced.

"Not much fun being yanked out of sleep in the middle of the night, is it?" Mom asked.

Dilly look confused. Then she slid down and pulled the blanket over her head. "No more," came her muffled voice. "I promise."

"Guess we taught her a lesson," I said as we headed back to bed.

The next morning we reminded Dilly of her promise. "That ends all of the midnight visits," Dad said sternly.

"OK," Dilly agreed. "Anyway, I have finished my experiment."

"But the experiment never worked," I said.

"Yes, it did. Last night I dreamed I was climbing a mountain. When you guys made all that racket, I thought it was an avalanche rumbling down the mountainside." Dilly smiled. "Now I can start my fitness experiment for phys. ed. I'll need someone to do sit-ups, someone to run in place, someone to jump—hey, where are all of you going?"

Where were we going? Out of the house. Maybe even out of the country. Anyplace to get away from Dilly's daffy projects.

The Worst Day in the World

By Gene Twaronite

Into every life a little rain must fall, but for Danny it was more like a downpour.

It wasn't just that bad things always happened to him. It was the *way* they happened. One rainy morning, for instance, he was walking to school when a passing car splashed him from head to toe with muddy water.

That would have been bad enough for most people, but when Danny went home to change clothes, he found the front door locked. So he climbed up the trellis to his bedroom window, which of course was also locked, and then up to the chimney, through which he squeezed and slid, getting covered with soot.

When he crawled out of the fireplace, his very own dog mistook him for a burglar and chased him all over the house, until Danny finally had to lock the dog in the bathroom. Then he changed his clothes and ran back to school where, just as he reached the front steps, he fell into a puddle the size of Lake Erie. And suddenly he remembered it was Saturday.

No matter how bad things got, though, Danny always managed to keep his chin up. He never lost hope that good things would someday come his way. "After all," he kept telling himself, "things can't get much worse."

But one day Danny had a *really* bad day. It was possibly the worst day anyone has ever had. It began first thing in the morning.

Unfortunately, he fell out of bed. Now, a lot of people fall out of bed occasionally, but it happened to Danny all the time.

Fortunately, Danny had learned to roll up like a ball to protect himself when he fell.

Unfortunately, this time he just rolled and bounced out of his bed, down the stairs, and through the front door, which, as luck would have it, had been left ajar.

Fortunately, Danny landed in an open garbage can filled with soft garbage.

Unfortunately, before anyone could see he was inside, the can was picked up and emptied into a garbage truck, which drove to the nearby landfill. There, as trucks roared and gulls swirled, Danny was dumped with the rest of the garbage into a big pit.

Fortunately, he landed on an old mattress.

Unfortunately, he was then covered with tons of sand and gravel, and more garbage.

Well, at least I won't have to go to school today, thought Danny. Then he took out his penknife and began to dig a tunnel. Hour after hour, Danny kept digging, and he would probably be digging to this very day.

But fortunately, an earthquake occurred nearby that opened a large crack in the earth's crust, into which Danny was dropped.

Unfortunately, like a great mouth, it swallowed up Danny and all the garbage without a trace.

For what seemed like eons Danny fell through layer after layer of multicolored rocks, until he splashed into an underground river.

Grabbing the knob of an old wooden door rushing by, Danny crawled on top and clung for dear life. He pulled a penlight from his pocket and looked around, as the river carried him through mile after mile of winding pink and purple caverns, where strange white fish leaped in the darkness. Finally, as rivers do, it flowed right into the sea.

Far beyond the coast Danny drifted on his sturdy wooden door. "It must be almost lunchtime," he said to himself. "I'm starved! But at least I won't have to eat that tuna casserole at school today." Danny hated tuna more than anything else.

Fortunately, he spotted an ocean liner on the horizon. Danny stood up and waved. Much to his surprise, the ship changed its course and headed straight for him. He was saved!

But unfortunately, at that moment, the ocean liner struck a giant iceberg that had broken off the coast of Greenland because of the earthquake.

Fortunately, all of the ship's passengers and crew members managed to jump onto lifeboats before the ship sank.

Unfortunately for Danny, he was caught up in the whirlpool and followed the ocean liner down to the bottom of the sea. There, in those dark blue waters, he might have remained for who knows how long.

For the first time that day, Danny started feeling sorry for himself. I am probably going to miss supper, he thought.

As he was thinking this, Danny was scooped up in the net of a passing tuna trawler. Though even the sea turtles and seals managed to escape the net, Danny was hauled in like all the unlucky fish. He was plopped into a hold filled with hundreds of flopping tuna. Then he was covered with ice and delivered to a nearby tuna cannery, where he was stuffed into a jumbo can marked Chunky Tuna and delivered to a local grocery store.

Fortunately, Danny's parents just happened to be out food shopping that very afternoon, and they just happened to buy the very can in which their son was packed. And because they were planning on having tuna casserole that night, they opened the can as soon as they got home. Much to their surprise, there was Danny, who, though somewhat squished and wrinkled, was none the worse for wear.

And after a warm bath and a nice big supper of pot roast—NO TUNA—Danny went up to bed and read himself to sleep with a rollicking good adventure story.

Miff and the Magnet

By Brenda Schneider

Professor Periwinkle peered through the round glasses perched on the end of his nose. "My, my, I really have done it this time. This is the best thing I have ever invented!" he said. "It's the world's most powerful electric magnet."

In the professor's hand was a small box, a little larger than a bar of soap. When the switch was turned on, the magnet pulled any metal object toward the box. No matter how large or heavy the object was, the little magnet could move it.

Suddenly, Professor Periwinkle's pet monkey ran into the room. "What monkey business have you been up to, Miff?" asked Professor Periwinkle.

Miff chattered loudly as he climbed up onto the professor's shoulder. He patted the professor's shiny bald head.

The professor got a nice red apple out of the cupboard for Miff. Miff really loved apples.

Ring, ring.

"Oh, my, there's the telephone," said the professor. He laid his magnet carefully on a shelf and hurried out of the room to answer the phone.

Miff jumped up to the shelf and picked up the funny little box. He examined it carefully. Then he hopped out the open window and scurried down the street carrying the box. As he ran, he began turning the switch on and off.

A lady came out of the beauty parlor with a lovely new hairdo. Just then Miff turned on the magnet. All the pins flew out of her curls. Her hair went *SPROING!* and stuck out just like a lot of springs. "Oh, you naughty little creature!" she yelled at Miff.

Miff kept right on playing with the magnet. Just as he turned it on again, a horse pulling a fruit cart came down the street. The magnet pulled off the horse's shoes. The horse reared up in surprise, and the fruit spilled on the ground. The fruit man yelled at Miff, too.

Cars stopped and honked. The fruit was blocking the street. A police officer came over to direct traffic. Miff turned on the magnet again, and it pulled the officer's whistle out of her mouth. Now the officer was angry, too. Miff wisely hurried on.

In the meantime, Professor Periwinkle returned to the laboratory to get his magnet. "It's gone," cried the professor, "and so is Miff. Oh, dear, oh, dear! What kind of monkey business is that monkey into now?" He ran outside to look for Miff.

Miff ran past a restaurant and turned on the magnet again. All the pots and pans came flying out the window. The cook came flying out, too. He began chasing the mischievous monkey. Miff did not turn off the magnet again. He just ran.

He ran past a wire fence, and the fence began to follow the cook who was chasing his pots and pans. Miff ran by a dog on a chain. The chain began following the fence, pulling the dog behind it. A boy on his bicycle rode over to see what all the fuss was about, and the magnet began pulling his bike. A manhole cover was pulled out of the street and rolled along with everything else. Miff and his metal menagerie ran past a woman mowing her lawn. The lawn mower followed the manhole cover. The woman ran after her lawn mower.

Just then the Professor came around the corner and saw Miff. "Miff, look! It's your favorite thing," he said, pulling an apple from his pocket.

Miff stopped running. All the metal things piled up against the magnet. When Miff reached out for the apple, the professor grabbed the magnet and turned it off.

The fence crumpled and fell down. The dog on the chain ran home yipping. The boy fell off his bike. The manhole cover rolled down the street. The woman ran up and grabbed her lawn mower.

To add to the confusion, the lady from the beauty parlor came running up the street, followed by the fruit man and the police officer.

Everyone was yelling at the same time. Just then the police officer found her whistle and blew it. Everyone became quiet. "Now, Professor," the officer said, "would you please explain what has been going on?"

"Oh, Officer, my pet monkey took my electric magnet and ran away with it. I'm so sorry, everyone! I will pay for anything that is broken."

When they reached home, Professor Periwinkle put his wonderful invention in a closet and locked the door. Next he found a long leash. He fastened one end to Miff's collar and the other end to his belt. "Now, you mischievous monkey, I will always know where you are."

Miff climbed up onto the professor's shoulder. He patted the professor's shiny bald head just as if nothing had happened.

The Rude Pinecone

By Elisabeth Nowlin

"Come in, Keith," Mrs. Happy said. "See the big pinecone I found in my yard? It looks so pretty on the table."

I looked, and there on the table was a full-grown porcupine staring at me. It twitched its nose and crossed its eyes.

"Is that a pinecone?" I asked.

"Oh yes, Keith," Mrs. Happy answered. "I lost my glasses, so I can't see very well but . . . yes, that's a pinecone."

My mamma taught me to be polite, so I didn't tell Mrs. Happy there was really a fat porcupine on her table. "Hello, porcupine," I whispered. "You're sitting on Mrs. Happy's table."

"She put me up here," the porcupine snapped. Then it stuck out its tongue. "Porcupines can't fly."

"You can talk?" I asked, scratching my head. I was very surprised.

The porcupine blinked its shiny black eyes. "I learned from a parrot. Didn't you know parrots talk? You aren't very smart!"

"Well, at least I'm polite," I said.

"Were you talking to me just now, Keith?" Mrs. Happy asked.

"No, Mrs. Happy," I said politely. "I'm talking to your pinecone."

Mrs. Happy laughed. "How funny you are. Always joking."

Just then the porcupine gave a loud yawn, stretched out on the tablecloth, and went to sleep.

"Even if you are sleepy, Keith," Mrs. Happy said, "it isn't polite to yawn."

By then I was *very* angry at the porcupine. I sat down and watched television. But it's hard to hear television over the snores of a sleeping porcupine. Mrs. Happy went to the kitchen to fix lunch. The porcupine woke up and yawned again.

"Is our lunch ready, Keith?" The porcupine looked at me and wiggled its toes.

"*Our* lunch?" I said. "You weren't asked to lunch." But someone was knocking, so I opened the door. "Come on in," I told my cousins, Anthony and Laurel and Steven. "Mrs. Happy is in the kitchen."

"Oh, look," cried Laurel. "How nice! A porcupine on the table!"

"Yes, I am beautiful," the porcupine said. It shook its sharp quills.

Steven stared. "It talks?"

"Yes," I answered. "It knows a parrot."

"I had a parrot," Steven told the porcupine. "It was big and yellow."

"Well, my friend is green," the porcupine said. "Personally, I don't like yellow parrots."

"Rude," said Steven.

Laurel laughed. "Isn't it cute? It looks just like a big pinecone."

"Welcome, dears," Mrs. Happy said. She carried in a big lemon cake. "Lunch will be ready soon. Children, have you seen the pinecone I found? I do so like a decorated table."

"Is that a pinecone?" Laurel asked. She had been taught to be polite also.

Anthony didn't say anything. I don't think he knew *what* to say. He would be in junior high school next year, and junior high school boys don't talk to porcupines.

"Now let's all sit down to our lunch," said Mrs. Happy. She put a big platter of hamburgers and a bowl of spinach on the table. "Oh dear, I forgot our noodle soup. Anthony, do be nice and bring in the soup. Hot soup always tastes so good, don't you think?"

"Yes," said Anthony.

"Yes," said the porcupine.

"Such good children," said Mrs. Happy.

Anthony put a cup of soup at each plate.

"Where's mine?" demanded the porcupine.

"Keith, don't complain," said Mrs. Happy with a frown. "There's enough for everyone."

The porcupine began eating my soup and got three noodles stuck in its quills. "Slurp, slurp, slurp," went the porcupine.

Steven was right. The porcupine was very rude.

Mrs. Happy laughed. "Aren't we having a fine and delicious lunch?"

"Yes," muttered the porcupine as it began eating Anthony's spinach.

"I won't share my spinach with a porcupine," said Anthony.

The porcupine burped loudly. Mrs. Happy glared at Anthony.

"I didn't say anything," Anthony told her.

"Manners, manners," said Mrs. Happy.

When we got to the cake, I could see that the porcupine loved it as much as I did. "This is my piece of cake," I said to it, "and I'm going to eat it myself!"

Mrs. Happy took a swallow of her milk. "We won't eat anything of yours, Keith. And who spilled noodles on my lovely pinecone? My, my!"

I started eating my cake, and the porcupine started eating my cake. We looked at each other nose to nose. I took a bite. Then the porcupine took a bite and dropped the cake crumbs all over Anthony's lap.

"Let me take these dishes into the kitchen," said Mrs. Happy.

The porcupine ate the last bit of the cake. "No more food!" it exclaimed. "Got to go, then." It hopped off the table and started out the door, leaving a trail of spinach and noodles.

"You're very rude," I told it. "And I don't care if it *is* rude to tell you that. Don't you have anything to say for yourself?"

"Yes," the porcupine answered. "Next time I want a glass of milk."

We were glad the porcupine was leaving. Laurel said she would pick Mrs. Happy a big bouquet of violets for the table instead. Violets don't eat spinach, and they don't talk back!

Buster Rabbit's Message from Space

By Elizabeth S. Chaffin

Thumpity-thump and *thumpity-thump!* Buster Rabbit bounced down the road, kicking up dust. Whoa! He slapped on his foot brake by the honeysuckle bush.

Mmmm! He just couldn't pass by without soaking up a headful of that honeysuckle sugar. So he closed his eyes a second to make his nose work better. But that was all the time it took for Mr. Fox to jump out of the bush, grab Buster Rabbit by the ears, and hold him up, kicking and squirming.

His hot breath on the back of Buster Rabbit's neck started Buster's thinker whirling.

"Hey, don't hold me by my ears," Buster demanded. "You're cutting off my communication."

"Your what?" Mr. Fox wanted to know.

"My communication. I've got a message coming in on my sky scanner," explained Buster Rabbit.

Mr. Fox shifted his hold to Buster Rabbit's neck, and Buster turned his ears this way and that, like a radar scanner scraping the sky.

"Yep, it's coming in loud and clear now. Message says they've run out of kings up there on Rabbit Planet and want to know if we have any to spare—and right away!"

Mr. Fox interrupted, "Well, I'm getting a message, too, but mine's from my stomach, saying it wants rabbit stew—and right away. Yes sir, rabbit stew tonight!" And the thought sent his heels clicking in the air.

"All right," said Buster Rabbit. "No need to tell you about those space rabbits who asked me to find them a king. I'm just getting a description of what they are looking for." Buster Rabbit twitched his ears again. "Prefer red color, sharp nose, bushy tail, extra smart."

"What, what?" Mr. Fox's ears shot up. "Hey, that kind of king sounds like me."

"But you wouldn't want to be a king," Buster Rabbit advised. "Nothing to do but sit on a throne with rabbits bowing all around you, waiting to bring anything you want. No, I'd better tell them to look somewhere else."

"Hold on there," said Mr. Fox. "It doesn't sound too bad to me."

"Well, then," said Buster Rabbit. "If you want them to pick you, we had better make you look like a king. Come on."

Buster Rabbit told Mr. Fox where to find the best throne-stump in the forest. He made him a scepter, which he explained was a long stick that kings are supposed to hold. And he stuck a turnip on the end to attract the rabbits. Then he made Mr. Fox a crown out of clay with shiny stones stuck in front.

All this wasn't easy to do with Mr. Fox still holding him around the neck and repeating every few minutes, "A rabbit in the hand is worth a hundred on another planet."

But when Mr. Fox sat on that throne-stump, holding his head up high so the sun would shine on his crown and twirling that turnip scepter in his hand, he looked like a proper king for sure.

"Oh, your majesty," cried Buster Rabbit with awe. "No rabbit in this world *or* outer space would fail to pick you for a king. But there is one little thing we overlooked. Rabbits would never choose a king who is holding another rabbit by the neck. Turn me loose so I can bow down in front of you."

Now Buster Rabbit knew that his rabbit-hole home was right beside the stump Mr. Fox was sitting on (which was the best reason he knew to have picked it for the throne). And, if his plans worked out, while Mr. Fox was watching for all those space rabbits, he would forget about one skinny little rabbit named Buster. Then Buster could slip into his hole quicker than you can say "turnip turnovers."

Well, Mr. Fox put him down, all right. But before Buster could scamper off—*kplop*—he was slammed to the ground and held flat by that turnip scepter.

"Thank you for making my turnip stick," laughed Mr. Fox. "It's especially handy for holding rabbits to their bowing bargains."

And he nudged Buster with the turnip scepter.

"I believe you said they would be here at three o'clock sharp," quoted Mr. Fox extra politely.

"Uh-huh," Buster Rabbit managed to grunt.

"Well, it's time for the countdown, and if those space rabbits don't show up, it's Buster stew with scepter turnip tonight!"

"10-9-8," he counted.

Buster began to wriggle. He couldn't budge to the right. He couldn't budge to the left. Or front or back and certainly not up.

"7-6-5," went the count.

All he could wriggle were his toes, so he put them into business, digging the only way they could—down. While his toes were digging, his mind was calculating. Which way to his hole? Maybe he could dig down to meet it if he could figure how far and which way. He decided to add 16 inches this way and divide by 2 (he always used numbers that come out even). He threw in some multiplying and lots of subtraction. With all this figuring, it came out that he should go by way of the square root.

He was on his way when he felt Mr. Fox punching around with his scepter. (Mr. Fox couldn't see much with the sun in his eyes.)

"Seems like you're getting smaller," said Mr. Fox.

"That's natural," Buster Rabbit managed to explain. "It's because you're getting the feel of being king. Other people always seem smaller to kings." He was steadily digging.

"4-3-2," Mr. Fox counted down.

"I think I hear them zooming in," said Buster Rabbit. "Sit up straight now, Mr. Fox."

When Mr. Fox sat up, Buster Rabbit's toes hit his hole and he went the other way—down. Down, down into his own safe, wonderful round little home.

The Screech

By Helen D. Harbor

My best friend, Betsy, is great in gymnastics. She can twist and bend as if her body were made out of putty. I look like a pretzel that was twisted wrong at the factory.

My mother says that I'm at the awkward stage because I'm growing so fast. I sure hope that she's right about that.

That's why I decided to become an actress.

It was Betsy's idea. "I'm going to help with the scenery for the school play, Maggie. Why don't you try out for a part?"

Mother and I talked it over. "What a great idea!" she said. "I used to love being in plays when I was in school. Tell you what. If you get a part, I'll even help you with your makeup."

Makeup! I didn't hear the rest of what she said. Imagine me with makeup on! I went to try out.

I couldn't wait to tell Mother the news. When she came home from work, I yelled, "I got a part in the play."

"I knew you could do it."

"Well, it's not really a speaking part, but it's a very important role," I told her.

"Oh?" Mother sat down.

"I screech and run off the stage." I rushed the words together.

"Screech?"

"It's sort of a scream, only it's a screech. When the play starts, I'm standing by a bus stop. I'm wearing a raincoat and holding an umbrella. The people behind the stage make a noise like a big clap of thunder. I try to open my umbrella, but it's stuck. Then the lights flash like lightning." I slowed down so she could get the picture.

"Then a man—that's Brian—touches my arm. Just when he does, there's a superloud clap of thunder. I screech and drop my umbrella."

Mother raised her eyebrows questioningly.

"I look scared to death when I run offstage. Mrs. Ruthe, the director, says my part is very important. It sets the mood for the whole play." I was out of breath.

Mother smiled. "I'm certain you'll do fine. We'll ask Aunt Tess and Caroline to come. They always ask us to Caroline's dance recitals."

My heart dropped right down to my feet. Caroline was so graceful. I just had to be good.

Mother might be certain I'd do fine, but I was beginning to wonder.

Finding a place to practice screeching wasn't easy. I was looking in the mirror in my bedroom, making a loud weird noise, when Mother came running in. "Maggie, what's wrong?"

"I'm practicing."

She sighed. "Of course. But please warn me the next time." On her way out she said, "Don't practice too much, dear. You might lose your voice."

All of a sudden I felt like an ice cube squeezed in the tray. I hadn't thought of that.

I went down in the basement to screech. My dog, Max, started howling and running around in circles. I even got into my closet. Mother thinks my closet is a mess when she is standing outside. I'm glad she never got inside. Inside it was dark, stuffy, and absolutely hopeless. It was too crowded in there to screech.

Walking home from school, I told Betsy, "I'm worried. What if I open my mouth and no noise comes out? What would I do?"

"Don't worry, Maggie. It'll work out." Betsy didn't look too sure to me.

At last the day of the play came. Aunt Tess and Caroline came, too.

Before the curtains opened, I felt sticky, like a half-eaten lollipop. My throat was dry. Betsy pushed the umbrella into my hand. Mrs. Ruthe smiled at me and said, "Good luck. Screech the best you can."

"Yes'm" was all I could say.

Then I was on the stage. The thunder clapped. The lightning flashed. I put my hand on the umbrella. Brian touched my arm. My hand was in the umbrella. I felt something—something slimy, like worms—something with legs that wriggled in my fingers.

I really screeched. Betsy stopped me when I ran off stage, or I would have run all the way home.

"Betsy! Betsy! The umbrella! There's something terrible in it!"

Betsy was grinning. "I'll bet that was the best screech any actress ever did."

"I don't care about the screech. Didn't you hear what I just said? There is something alive in the umbrella."

Betsy burst out laughing. Tears rolled down her face, and she grabbed her stomach.

"Betsy, you put something in the umbrella!" I couldn't believe it.

"It was only a creepy rubber spider. I'm sorry that I scared you so badly, but you were so worried you'd lose your voice. I wanted to make sure you screeched."

I was starting to get really furious at Betsy when Mrs. Ruthe came over and put her arms around me. "You were wonderful, Maggie. Why, you looked as if you were going to jump out of your skin. That's what I call acting."

Even Aunt Tess and Caroline hugged me. Mother did, too. I think Mother was glad I was through with all of my practicing.

I thanked Betsy, and we both laughed really hard. "Next time I hope you get a speaking part," she said.

"Me, too."

But I'll always wonder what would have happened if I didn't have such a smart friend.

Robert Floogle's Kugel

By Margaret Springer

Robert Floogle tiptoed out of his room. He looked both ways. Mom and Dad were not in the hallway. "Come on," he hissed to his big brother, Joe. "You can bring your book."

They crept silently into the kitchen and closed the door. Only the cat was there, curled up and looking at them sleepily.

"Now what's this all about?" asked Joe.

Robert was putting on Papa's apron. "Simple," he said. "It's their anniversary, right? I am going to make the most yummy, the most scrumptious, the most imaginative, and the most mouth-watering lunch the world has ever tasted."

"Oh, no!" said Joe.

"Oh, yes!" said Robert. He waved a wooden spoon near Joe's nose. "You don't know this, Joe, but someday I'll be a famous chef."

"Robert Floogle, Master Chef," said Joe. "The world isn't ready, Robert."

"I'll be known as Mister Roberto," said Robert.

Joe shook his head. "OK, Mister Roberto," he said. "But where do I come in?"

"Nowhere," said Robert. "But they won't let me cook by myself. So you sit there and finish your book, and I'll tell you if I need help."

Suddenly Mom came into the kitchen. "What's this Mister Roberto stuff?" she asked.

"Mom!" said Robert. "Out! Out!"

"Sorry," said Joe. "You're not allowed in. Mister Roberto, the world-famous chef, is going to make lunch today."

"Oh, my," said Mom, looking worried. "Uh . . . that's nice, Robert." She tried her best to sound pleased. "I hope," she added.

She went into the living room and told Dad.

"Oh, no," said Dad.

"He means well," said Mom.

Mom and Dad and Joe loved Robert very much. But they did *not* love his cooking. He was a very creative cook. He didn't pay much attention to cookbooks or ingredients.

"Remember last year's birthday cake, Robert," called Mom from the living room.

"Yes, Mom," said Robert, grating potatoes and carrots into a bowl. He remembered. The cake had been perfect. But not the frosting! He'd put in oil instead of butter. Well, Mister Roberto had to start somewhere, even if Mom's candles fell over in the runniest, funniest frosting that the world had ever seen.

Joe was busy reading. The cat yawned, sat up, and watched Robert.

"Remember the picnic, Robert," called Dad.

"Yes, Dad," said Robert, stirring in milk and eggs. He remembered. It had been a wonderful picnic. He had made creative and nutritious sandwiches. A choice of sauerkraut and cream cheese, peanut butter with relish, or tuna with onion and ketchup. It wasn't his fault if no one was hungry.

Splat!

"Whoops!" said Robert. "I dropped an egg." The cat had streaked into the living room. "It's OK, though," he added. "I missed the cat." He cleaned up the floor. "Now, where was I?"

Joe looked up from his book. "Remember the Christmas eggnog, Robert," he said.

"Yes, Joe," said Robert, stirring in some grated cheese. He remembered. Christmas eggnog was his specialty. He made it when the relatives had come to visit. He told them he had not meant to use cayenne pepper instead of nutmeg. It wasn't his fault if they didn't believe him.

Today Robert was very careful. He looked at the labels as he shook in salt and pepper and onion powder.

Mom and Dad and the cat heard all kinds of interesting noises coming from the kitchen. The clatter of cutlery. Things going in and out of cupboards and drawers. The fridge door opening and closing. Water running at the kitchen sink. Bowls and pans being moved around.

Finally, Robert put something in the oven very carefully. He took a clean tablecloth and set the table. He added his ivy plant for a centerpiece. He poured the milk and set out a basket of rolls and a big salad. Later he took an unusual-looking casserole from the oven.

"Lunchtime!" called Robert.

Joe finished his book and stretched. "Something *smells* good, anyway," he said.

Mom and Dad came into the kitchen. The cat did not.

"Well, doesn't it *look* nice," said Mom uneasily.

"Yes. Robert certainly works hard when he cooks," said Dad anxiously.

There was a worried silence while Dad served the casserole.

Mom tasted a tiny nibble from her plate. She made a face and looked puzzled. "Why, Robert," she said. "It's—it's good!"

Dad tasted a bigger forkful. "Son," he said, "it's *more* than good. It's delicious!"

Robert smiled. "Surprise!" he said proudly. "And happy anniversary."

Joe was almost finished with his serving. "This is great, man!" he said. "What is it?"

Robert wanted to tell his family that it was the most yummy, the most scrumptious, the most imaginative, and the most mouth-watering lunch the world had ever tasted. But he didn't.

"It's potato kugel," he said. "I got it right out of a book."

Exactly
the Truth

By Sandy Landsman

"What do you mean, it's lost?"

"I lost it, that's all. I just lost it!"

"Great!"

"I put it down for only a minute!"

Karen sat on the sidewalk. "That's great," she repeated. "That's just great!"

"Will you stop saying that?" Angrily, Bob kicked at a stone.

"I'll say it all I want, if I want to! It's great, great, great, great, great!"

"I *said* I was sorry."

"Wonderful."

At least she hadn't said "great" again. Bob sat down beside her.

"You looked all over?"

"Everywhere!"

Karen groaned. "What did you have to go and lose it for?"

Bob didn't answer.

"Dad will be furious!"

Bob nodded. As a rule, Professor Nathan was pretty even-tempered with his children. But then again, they had never before lost his brand-new, just-completed Veritographer—the truth-detecting device that their father had spent months inventing.

"He said it was the most important thing he ever invented," said Karen. "It was supposed to teach people to always say the exact truth."

"I know," said Bob.

"Oh, I never should have pestered Dad to lend it to us! I should have known something like this would happen!"

Bob scuffed his shoes nervously. "I wanted to use it only once, just to show up that Donny Parker for always telling lies about people. You know what he said this morning? He said that Mr. Frankel wears a wig!"

"Wow! Did the machine start beeping and catch him up?"

"No." Bob half-smiled. "Wouldn't you know it? This once he was telling the truth!"

"It figures," said Karen. "Show me where you lost it."

"You're sure it was right here?" Karen scanned the park.

"Positive! I just put it down on the grass for a second while I watched the baseball game. Then when I turned around, it was gone."

"Was anyone around?"

"Not really."

"*Think,* Bob. Come *on!*"

"Well—just some little kid with a red wagon. His mother told him to pick up his toys and come along with her."

Bob and Karen looked at each other.

"Hey, you don't think . . . ," Bob began.

"It's got to be! The kid must have picked up the Veritographer along with his toys and dumped it in his wagon! Did you see which way they went?"

Bob tried to remember. "No," he said at last, "but look at that—wheel marks!"

Not two feet from where Karen was standing, the wagon wheels had left a trail in the dirt.

"Let's go!" cried Karen.

They tore off, following the trail. It wound around trees and behind the swings and came out at last near the jungle gym.

"Oh, no!" cried Karen. She stopped short.

Bob saw it the same moment she did. The trail led straight to the sandbox.

"I don't believe it!" said Bob as he looked down into the sand.

"Believe it," said Karen.

There in the sand was the impression of a small box with buttons and a beeper. Someone had been using the Veritographer as a sandbox toy!

Bob and Karen dug up the whole sandbox. But no luck. The Veritographer was gone.

"We've *got* to find it now!" said Bob. "If we don't find it right away and get it home and clean it out, the whole thing will be ruined!"

"I know," said Karen glumly. "Got any ideas?"

Bob shook his head. Two trails led from the sandbox. One trail had been left by the wagon; the other seemed to have been left by a tricycle. Both disappeared where they met the pavement.

Bob stared at the paved area. Many kids were playing and riding across it. Every minute new kids rode into the area and other kids rode away.

"There's no way we can ever find it now!"

Beep beep. A soft sound came from somewhere in the park.

Karen tried to brush the sand off her jeans. There was sand in her clothes, sand under her nails, even sand in her hair. "And it's all your fault," she declared. "Nobody else's. It's entirely, completely, one hundred percent your fault, Bob!"

BEEP BEEP. The sound came louder.

"What's that?" asked Bob.

Karen stopped short. "It's the Veritographer! It's beeping because I said things that weren't exactly the truth!"

"Which way was the sound coming from?"

"I don't know!" said Karen. "It has stopped."

Bob thought fast and said, "My head is bigger than a giant watermelon."

BEEP BEEP! came the sound.

"Over this way!" called Karen. "I'm seventy years old!"

BEEP BEEP!

"The sound moved a little to the side! And it's getting softer!"

Bob and Karen ran onto the pavement, following the sound.

"Let's try for a loud one!" called Karen.

"I live on the moon!" shouted Bob. "And I eat green cheese and moonbeams for breakfast!"

BEEP BEEP BEEP!

"And I go to school on Mars and fly back and forth on a jelly bean!"

BEEP BEEP BEEP BEEP BEEP!

"There it is!" cried Karen.

A little boy on a tricycle was riding back and forth through the park. A toy pail hung from the handlebars, and from inside the pail came the sound of the Veritographer.

"I see," said Professor Nathan, when Bob and Karen had finished telling him their story. "I'm glad you told me."

"We thought of just cleaning it out and giving it back without saying anything," said Karen.

Bob nodded. "But that would have been almost like lying."

"You're right," said the professor. "Well, you've shown me one thing. I can count on *you* two kids, with or without the Veritographer."

"Thank you," said Bob and Karen.

Professor Nathan beamed. "Because, no matter what, my children would never *ever* say anything but exactly the truth. Right, kids?"

"Right!" said Bob.

"Right!" said Karen.

Beep beep! went the Veritographer.

Getting Rosie's Rooster

By Eve Bunting

"Cock-a-doodle-doo!"

Rosie's rooster sang out across its own backyard. Its voice jumped a vacant lot, right into Mr. Hickman's bedroom.

Mr. Hickman glared at his clock. "Five A.M. That rooster has to go. It simply has to go."

Mr. Hickman said most things twice, even when he talked to himself. It added punch, he thought. A lot of punch.

He got up, dressed, and headed straight for Rosie's house.

A very tall, very red-haired woman opened the door. Rosie.

"No one could sleep with that dreadful noise," Mr. Hickman said. "Your rooster simply has to go."

"And where is my rooster to go, pray tell, since this is his home and the law lets me keep him? Are you suggesting roast rooster?"

"I'm suggesting a place in the country, a home on the farm," Mr. Hickman said.

"My hens would die of a broken heart. So would I. I'm sorry," Rosie closed the door gently. But firmly.

"Cock-a-doodle-doo!" the rooster jeered.

"Well," Mr. Hickman said. "Well!"

There was another house partway up the road.

"We must all complain about that wretched rooster," he told the little man who opened the door. "Then she'll have to get rid of it."

The little man's face turned purple. "That rooster takes me back to my boyhood on the farm, sir. It reminds me of sun in the cottonwoods. Get rid of Rosie's rooster? Never." He didn't close the door as gently as Rosie had closed hers.

"Well! Well!" Mr. Hickman headed for the house across the street.

The girl running across the front yard looked so healthy that Mr. Hickman felt ill. Her legs pumped up and down as Mr. Hickman talked, as if standing still was a waste of their time.

"I *love* Rosie's rooster. He wakes me with the sun. Get rid of Rosie's rooster? Never." And she was gone.

"Cock-a-doodle-doo!"

Mr. Hickman gritted his teeth. That rooster was thumbing its beak at him.

As soon as he got home, he made a call to a man he knew who owned a farm.

"How long will you want me to board the rooster?" the farmer asked.

"It will be a permanent visitor," Mr. Hickman said. "Very permanent."

When it was dark, Mr. Hickman got a box and a flashlight. He squeezed through his back hedge and crossed the vacant lot, where a sign said PRIVATE PROPERTY: KEEP OUT. There was Rosie's fence. Mr. Hickman switched off his flashlight. He dropped the light and the box over the fence onto Rosie's grass. He took another step . . . and the ground cracked under him.

He was falling, falling, feet first, the way someone jumps into a swimming pool.

"What . . . ? Where . . . ?" Mr. Hickman was wedged in a narrow hole, no wider than he was. His head poked out, and above him he could see the night sky, salted with stars.

"Help!" Mr. Hickman shouted. He added another "Help!" for extra punch.

But no one came.

Surely someone would find him in the morning. But maybe not. This was PRIVATE PROPERTY: KEEP OUT.

"Oh, my," Mr. Hickman said. "Oh, my."

The night seemed to last as long as ten nights. But at last, through the gray light of dawn, he saw a corner of Rosie's henhouse. Next he saw Rosie's rooster flutter onto the roof and stretch its neck.

"Cock-a-doodle-doo!"

Never had there been such a heavenly sound.

"Rooster?" Mr. Hickman called. "Get Rosie!"

The rooster's head cocked. It flew out of Mr. Hickman's sight, and then it came to stand in front of him.

"Get Rosie, Rooster!" Mr. Hickman begged.

There was a flurry of feathers, and now Rooster was perched on top of Mr. Hickman's head.

"Cock-a-doodle-doo!" It dug its toes into Mr. Hickman's head.

Somewhere, far away, a voice called, "Rooster? Where are you?"

"Help! Help!" Mr. Hickman called, as loud as he possibly could.

"Cock-a-doodle-doo!" Rosie's rooster repeated.

There was the sound of feet in dry leaves. Then Rosie was staring down at him.

"Rooster!" she gasped. "What are you doing on Mr. Hickman's head? That's no way to make him like you!" She picked up Rooster.

"Are you down there for a reason, Mr. Hickman?" Rosie asked.

"No reason," Mr. Hickman said. "I fell. I simply fell in."

He hoped Rosie wouldn't ask what he was doing when he fell in. She didn't.

"I told the owner of this lot there would be an accident one day. If you'll excuse me, I'll call the fire department to get you out of that hole."

The fire fighters put a rope around Mr. Hickman and lifted.

"If that rooster hadn't found you . . . ," one of them said.

Mr. Hickman did not like unfinished sentences. But this one had punch. A lot of punch.

He stroked Rooster's silky feathers. "Thank you," he said.

"Cock-a-doodle-doo!"

"Would earplugs help, Mr. Hickman?" Rosie asked. "I'd be glad to buy them."

Mr. Hickman smiled. "Certainly not. I love to hear him. A heavenly call that rooster has. Absolutely heavenly."

FROG LEGS FOR LUNCH

By Joan Knaub

"He's great, but you should have brought him in a cage," Billy Clark said, admiring the large spotted bullfrog in his friend's hand.

"I just forgot," Joe Gillan admitted. "I'll get a box from the science teacher after recess."

But when the boys got back to class, Miss Watson, their teacher, was waiting for them. "We will spend the rest of the school day in the library," she told them. "We're giving achievement tests. Hurry on down, please, so that we can get started."

"Pssst, what about him?" Billy worried, pointing to the frog Joe still carried.

Smiling, Joe plopped the frog into the nearest drinking fountain. "I'll get him when we come back," he explained. "He'll be fine here."

Meanwhile, Scott Smathers was yawning in art class. The assignment was to draw something in the school that interested him, and so far he hadn't had a single idea.

"May I get a drink of water, please, Miss Hazel," he asked the art teacher.

"Of course, Scott." Miss Hazel smiled. "Maybe you'll get an inspiration at the same time."

Even so, Miss Hazel was surprised to see Scott return to his seat and begin drawing so earnestly. Curious as to what prompted such enthusiasm, she walked behind him.

"Now, Scott," she said gently, "the assignment was to draw something you have seen in school. There has never been, to my knowledge, a frog in the drinking fountain."

"There is now," Scott said cheerfully.

Naturally, Miss Hazel had to check, and when she bent over the fountain—

"Urk!" said the bullfrog, springing past Miss Hazel's startled face.

"Eck!" squealed Miss Hazel.

"Glurk!" answered the bullfrog, heading down the hall in a series of neat, dignified hops.

"Really, Miss Hazel," complained Mr. Hacker, the principal, coming around the corner with a frown on his face.

Miss Hazel pointed a trembling finger down the hall where the frog was just disappearing into the music room.

Mr. Hacker and a timid Miss Hazel hurried after the frog. When they got to the music room, Mr. Britting was standing with his baton in the air and a startled look on his face.

The frog hopped nimbly across the drum—BOOM!—across the cymbals—CLANG-CLANK!—across the piano—TINKLELY, TINKLELY, THUNK!—and out the door.

As Miss Hazel followed Mr. Hacker and the frog, she heard Mr. Britting say, "I rather liked that last arrangement. Shall we play it once more?"

The frog headed for the gym, and once inside he was surrounded by boys and girls doing exercises. Mrs. Willoughby, the physical education teacher, was saying, "I want to see more pep, boys and girls. Look alive. One, two! One, two!"

Just then, the frog hopped on Judy Jameson's back. She leaped up in a hurry.

"Good, Judy," called Mrs. Willoughby. "That's just what I meant."

The frog went past Buzz Mackey's knee, and he was so startled he kicked his foot straight up in the air.

"Fine, Buzz, fine. Keep up the good work." It was plain that Mrs. Willoughby was as pleased as punch with their performance.

The frog leaped past the Paxon twins, who stood up like soldiers on parade.

"Oh, class, I'm so glad to see such improvement," Mrs. Willoughby was saying as the frog hopped out the door.

"The cafeteria! He's headed for the cafeteria," Miss Hazel gasped as she tried to keep up with Mr. Hacker. When the two of them reached the cafeteria door, they looked in on a scene of total confusion at the lunch tables.

The third-graders were eating lunch, and the frog had splashed through a bowl of chili, waded through a platter of potatoes, and overturned a dish of apricots. The kids were staring in complete amazement, and the teacher on lunch duty looked glassy-eyed.

Only the cook was not too stunned to move. Grabbing a large strainer, she popped it over the frog as he rested for a moment on the edge of the serving counter.

"Gotcha!" she grinned. "And now, who'd like a plate of frog legs for lunch?"

Of course, the frog did not really end up on the lunch menu. He was given a cozy wire cage for the rest of the day and released at the edge of a swampy pond after school.

But that wasn't quite the end of the story. Scott Smathers won first place in the City Schools Art Contest for his picture of a frog sitting in a drinking fountain.

And Joe Gillan caused quite a stir in class the next day when he complained about the frog in his throat.

Still, it was Mr. Hacker who had the final say.

"I think," he announced in weekly assembly, "that every school should have at least one frog somewhere—just to keep things hopping!"

KING DOUGHNUT

By Pamela Miller

Not so long ago in a happy kingdom lived a king who loved doughnuts. He had a doughnut after breakfast, a doughnut after lunch, and another after dinner. How sweet and good they were.

As time went on, the king began to order two doughnuts after every meal, then three, then four. Finally he had a whole plateful after each meal!

The king grew so fond of doughnuts that he thought, why not have doughnuts instead of my meals? So he ate doughnuts *instead* of his breakfast, *instead* of his lunch, and *instead* of his dinner. And he had doughnuts *after* his breakfast, *after* his lunch, and *after* his dinner . . . until he was eating doughnuts all day long! Plate after plate was piled high with doughnuts. There seemed to be no end to his eating.

The king required such a great supply of doughnuts each day that all the farms in his kingdom had to become bakeries. All the shops became bakeries, too. All the people became bakers. The happy kingdom was not so happy anymore. For it took mountains of doughnuts to feed the king each day.

One morning the king awoke feeling very poorly. He looked in the mirror and found that he had grown to such a tremendous size that he couldn't see all of himself in the mirror at one time, no matter where he stood in his huge room.

"Call my advisors!" the king demanded. "I do not feel well, and I do not look well."

After breakfast the king greeted his first advisor. "Your Majesty," said the advisor, "I have the answer to your problem. If a person looks well, he feels well. The answer is stripes! Striped clothing will make you look slimmer, then you will feel better."

The king ordered a striped suit to be made and brought to him. But after putting it on, he felt no better. And he still could not see all of himself in the mirror.

"Call in another advisor," commanded the king. "I do not feel well, and I do not look well."

After lunch the king welcomed his second advisor. "I have the answer," said the second advisor. "What you need is exercise. I suggest you try standing on your head several times each day."

With much difficulty, a lot of groaning, and a good deal of help from the guards, the king managed to stand on his head. But when the guards let go, he came down with a crash. "This will never do!" cried the king. "Send in my third advisor after dinner. For I do not feel well, and I do not look well."

"I have the answer," said the third advisor as the king finished his plateful of doughnuts. "What you need is a bicycle. Riding a bicycle will give you right-side-up exercise, not upside-down-standing-on-your-head exercise."

The king ordered a special royal bicycle to be made. It had to be very strong and very large. Unfortunately, the bike was so heavy the king couldn't move it an inch. Sadly, the king climbed down off the bike.

"I have no more advisors," he said. "Tell the people of my kingdom that anyone who can advise me how I might feel better and look better will be greatly rewarded."

Everyone had an idea for the king. One person suggested warm baths. Another thought cold baths. Someone suggested that the king get more sleep. Someone else thought less sleep. One person suggested the king get a pet. Another proposed that he learn to play an instrument. Many tried to cheer the king with their dancing. There were even jugglers. But nothing worked.

Someone suggested that a vacation might be the answer. So the king set off in his royal carriage, accompanied by all of his best royal doughnut bakers. A week later the king returned home. He looked miserable and felt even worse.

Then one morning, just as the king sat down to his usual heap of doughnuts for breakfast, a guard came in with a message. "There is a very young baker here to see you. He says he knows what you can do to feel better and look better. He's only a boy. Shall I send him away?"

"No, no," said the king. "Let him in."

"What would you advise?" asked the king.

"The answer is very simple," said the boy. "STOP EATING DOUGHNUTS."

"Stop eating doughnuts?" repeated the king. "What an unhappy idea. But I'll try anything. For I do not feel well, and I do not look well. Send back that plate of doughnuts," ordered the king.

From that day on, the king began eating well-balanced meals. He had no stack of doughnuts *instead* of each meal. He had no stack of dough-nuts *after* each meal.

Each day he felt better. Each day he looked better . . . until one day, he looked into the mirror. He could see all of himself at one time. He wasn't enormous anymore. He was healthy and fit.

"Bring that young baker to me," commanded the king. "I want to thank him for advising me so very wisely."

"How can I reward you?" the king asked the boy. "Anything you want you shall have. For I feel well, and I look well."

"Well," said the boy, "before my family's farm was turned into a bakery, I was a farm boy. I would like to be a farm boy again, and I would like my father to be a farmer."

"Yes, yes," said the king. "Why didn't I think of that? All the farms shall be farms again. All the shops shall be shops again. And all the people shall return to their jobs. We will not be needing all those doughnut bakers anymore."

Home Sweet Madhouse

By Harriett Diller

I sent Mom upstairs for a nap before the real estate lady came. "You need it," I said. "You were up all night with the baby."

"Are you sure, Jake? Those people are coming to see the house in an hour." Mom sighed. "And we have *got* to sell this house, so we can join Dad on the coast."

"Don't worry, Mom. I've got everything under control. We'll keep the house nice."

"We" meant Felicia and Sam and the dog and me. The baby couldn't mess up much from his crib.

I found Felicia and Sam in the kitchen. They were sitting at the table.

"I'm playing quiet," Felicia said.

"Me, too," Sam said.

"Can we play Dragonland?" Felicia asked.

I shook my head. "Every time that you both play Dragonland you leave plastic dragons on the floor. People step on them and hurt their feet."

The doorbell rang. "Stay put," I told Sam and Felicia as I jogged to answer it.

A guy smiled at me from the front porch. "Good afternoon, sir. I represent Little Einstein, Incorporated. If you'll give me just a few minutes of your time, I'll show you how to raise your child's IQ."

"No thanks."

"For only pennies a day—"

"No thanks." I inched the door shut and hurried back to the kitchen.

Felicia and Sam weren't sitting anymore. They were standing on the kitchen chairs. Sam watched while Felicia poured grape juice from a huge pitcher into two toy teacups.

"We're having a tea party," Sam said. "Felicia's the mommy and daddy. I'm the little boy."

"Felicia, stop!" I yelled.

Too late. The cups overflowed, and there was grape juice all over Mom's best white tablecloth—the one she put there so the kitchen would look nice for the house buyers. I moved the teacups and pitcher. I grabbed the tablecloth and crammed it into the washer.

"Mom says grape stains are the worst. I'll use lots of detergent." I measured four cups of the stuff and dumped them all into the washer. "That'll get the stain out," I told Sam and Felicia. Only they weren't there to hear me.

"Felicia! Sam! Where are you?" I heard giggles in the living room.

"Felicia's riding a horsey," Sam chanted.

Felicia's horsey was the dog. The dog barked.

"Felicia!" I yelled. "Get off that dog!"

I ran to the kitchen to answer the ringing phone.

"Good afternoon, sir," a man's voice said. "I represent the Four Seasons Window Company. If you'll give me just a few minutes of—"

"No thanks."

"For only pennies a day—"

"No thanks!" I hung up.

Now the baby was crying. Sam was crying, too.

"Stop it, Felicia!" he said.

Crash!

Felicia and Sam and a lamp ended up together on the living room floor.

"What's going on?" I said.

"Championship wrestling," Felicia told me. "I'm Meany Maloney. Sam is Cowardly Clyde. Do you want to be referee?"

"No, I don't want—"

The phone rang again.

"Good afternoon. I represent the Atlas Fitness Club. If you'll give me just a few minutes—"

I slammed the receiver back on the hook just as the doorbell rang. "If this is another salesman—"

Felicia got there before I did. "It's three salesmen!" she yelled.

"Three!" Then I saw who it really was.

It was the real estate lady with the house buyers. Early. The baby was still crying. The lamp was still on the floor. And now the Dragonland game was open on the sofa.

"Come in!" I yelled above the baby's crying.

"The Colvers want to see your house," the real estate lady said.

The baby stopped crying, just in time for everybody to hear the washer throwing a fit. We all rushed to the kitchen and watched suds and water pour over the sides of the washer.

"Water slide!" Felicia said and slid gleefully across the wet floor.

Mom staggered into the kitchen, rubbing her eyes. "What on earth is going on?" she mumbled.

I gave her the baby. "Would you show them the house?" I said. "I've got everything under control."

By the time they came back, I did. The Colvers even mentioned how nice and shiny the kitchen floor looked.

"Come into the living room and sit down," Mom told the grownups.

Mr. Colver sat on the sofa. "Owowowowow!"

"My dragons!" Felicia scolded him. "You sat on my dragons."

I groaned. "Felicia. I told you not—"

"We didn't leave them on the floor. We left them on the *sofa,*" she said.

The real estate lady gave us a look that said, "You expect me to sell this house?" And I certainly couldn't blame her.

Mr. Colver looked at his wife. "You thinking what I'm thinking?"

She smiled. "That this place feels just like home?"

"Exactly. All the other places we visited today were too perfect. We couldn't imagine our kids living there. But this place . . . it's a real home."

"Is that what it is?" I asked. "I thought it was a disaster area!" Everybody laughed, even Mom and the real estate lady.

The Wonderful Taker-Awayer

By Lee Priestley

Libby's mother planted the last tulip bulb
beside the front walk. Then she waded through
the red and brown leaves to the front door.

"Hardly able to get through!" she grumbled.
"When are you going to rake up those leaves in
the yard, Libby?"

"I'm thinking about a better way to move
leaves," Libby said.

Her mother sighed. "Such peculiar things happen when *you* start thinking, Libby." Then she
went indoors.

Libby kept on thinking. Her invention should first scoop up the leaves. Then it should deliver them into the trash container. Libby studied the old furnace pipes the repairmen had piled in the alley. If she could hook up those pipes to her mother's vacuum cleaner . . .

Libby invented a Taker-Awayer. First she joined the furnace pipes until they reached the trash container in the alley. Then she put wheels under the pipes. She added a gadget and a gismo. She spliced in her mother's vacuum cleaner. Then she crossed her fingers and flicked the switch.

Rrrhhhuuumm . . . sw-oo-sh! The Taker-Awayer gulped a big pile of leaves.

Libby shut it off and ran back to the alley. A last red leaf fluttered out of the old furnace pipes. The trash container was half full. Her invention was really working!

In no time Libby moved all the leaves from the front yard. But when she reached to switch off the machine, she stumbled—and the Taker-Awayer became a Runner-Awayer!

Rrrhhhuuumm . . . sw-oo-sh! It flew around the yard with Libby chasing after it. The Taker-Awayer began taking other things besides leaves. It scooped the rows of tulip bulbs Mother had planted beside the front walk. Then it sucked the water out of the lily pool. It was reaching for the laundry on the backyard clothesline when Libby caught it.

Libby turned off the Taker-Awayer. "Now what?" she muttered.

But inventors seldom run out of ideas. Right away Libby saw that she must create a new invention, a Putter-Backer.

So she connected this, and she disconnected that. She took off a gismo and put on a gadget. Then she crossed her fingers for luck and flipped the switch again.

Rrrhhhuuumm . . . sw-oo-sh! Red and brown leaves blew back over the front yard. Libby tried to aim the tulip bulbs back into their rows. The water from the lily pool flew through the air just as Mother came out the front door.

"My goodness!" Mother said. "A shower and not a cloud in the sky! And leaves everywhere. Libby, *when* are you going to rake?"

"Right now, Mother," said Libby meekly.

She decided not to use the Taker-Awayer again until she had improved it. She moved all the leaves from the front yard to the trash bin in the alley the old-fashioned way . . . with a rake. It took the rest of the afternoon.

When spring comes, Libby's mother will be very surprised. Tulips blossoming in the lily pool! Water lilies growing beside the front walk!

But it won't surprise Libby.